MARC BROWN

ARTHUR'S TEACHER TROUBLE

PICTURE CORGI BOOKS

Also available by Marc Brown, and published by Picture Corgi Books:
ARTHUR'S CHRISTMAS
ARTHUR'S TOOTH
WITCHES FOUR

ARTHUR'S TEACHER TROUBLE

A CORGI BOOK   0 552 525081

Originally published in U.S.A. by The Atlantic Monthly Press.
First published in Great Britain by Piccadilly Press Ltd.

PRINTING HISTORY
Piccadilly Press edition published 1987
Picture Corgi edition published 1989

Picture Corgi Books are published by Transworld Publishers Ltd., 61-63 Uxbridge Road, Ealing, London W5 5SA, in Australia by Transworld Publishers (Australia) Pty. Ltd., 15-23 Helles Avenue, Moorebank, NSW 2170, and in New Zealand by Transworld Publishers (N.Z.) Ltd., Cnr. Moselle and Waipareira Avenues, Henderson, Auckland.

Made and printed in Portugal by Printer Portugesa

The bell rang.

The first day of school was over.

Kids ran out of every classroom – every one but Room 13.

Here, the children filed out slowly, in alphabetical order.

"See you tomorrow," said their teacher, Mr Ratburn.

"I can't believe he gave us homework the first day," said Arthur.
"I had the Rat last year," said Prunella. "Boy, do I feel sorry for you!"

"Make one wrong move," warned Binky Barnes, "and he puts you on death row."

"He's really a vampire with magical powers," said Chris.

As everyone was leaving, the headmaster came out of his office. "It may be the first day, but don't forget the Summer spellathon," he reminded them. They all groaned.

"Mr Ratburn's class has won it every year," the head continued. Mr Ratburn's new class cheered.

"If I win again this year do I get my name on the trophy twice?" asked Prunella.

"Not if I can help it," whispered Francine.

When Arthur got home, he slammed the back door.
"How was school?" Mother asked.
"I got the strictest teacher in the whole world,"
grumbled Arthur.

"Have a chocolate biscuit," said Mother.
"Don't have time," said Arthur. "I have tons of homework."
"I'll eat Arthur's," said D.W. "I don't have any homework."
"You don't even go to school," said Arthur.
"I know," D.W. smiled.

After dinner Arthur was still doing homework.
"What's that?" asked D.W.
"It's a map of Africa," said Arthur.
"Looks like a mushroom pizza," said D.W. "Next year when I'm in the infants I won't have *any* homework. Ms Meeker never gives it."
"Mum!" called Arthur. "D.W.'s being a pest."
"Time for bed," said Mother. "You can finish your map of Florida in the morning."
"Africa," sighed Arthur.

The next day, Mr Ratburn announced a spelling test for every Friday. "I want you to study very hard," he said. "Each test will have a hundred words." Buster looked pale.

"And at the end of this year," continued Mr Ratburn, "the two students who have the highest scores will represent our class at the all-school spellathon."

Each week everyone in Arthur's class studied harder than ever. Arthur spent a lot of time avoiding D.W. and looking for quiet places to study.

All that year Muffy, Francine, the Brain and Arthur had very close scores. Eventually, it was time for the final test. Arthur could hear Mrs Fink's class leaving for a trip to the aquarium. "Why did we have to get stuck with the Rat?" he whispered to Francine.

Mr Ratburn corrected their papers during lunch. "Class," he said, "most of you did very well this year. But on this test only two of you spelled *every* word correctly."

Muffy smiled. Francine hiccupped.

Buster patted his good luck charm.

Mr Ratburn cleared his throat.

"Our class representatives for the spellathon will
be the Brain and Arthur."
"There must be some mistake!" said Muffy.

Mr Ratburn gave Arthur and the Brain each a
special list of words. "Just study these and you'll
be ready for the spellathon in two weeks," he said.

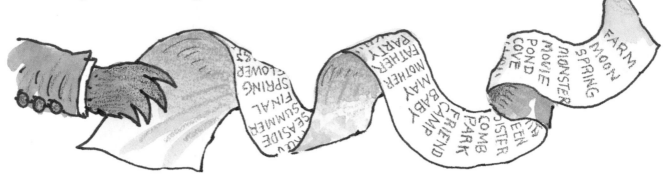

Arthur's family helped him study.
Grandma asked Arthur
his spelling words.

"Have you cut the L-A-W-N?" Father asked.
"Have you made your B-E-D?" Mother added.

D.W. helped too.
When Francine and Buster came over to play,
D.W. answered the door.
"Arthur can't play, but I can," she said. "I don't
have to study."

"I can't believe the spellathon is finally here," said Grandma.
"Good luck, Arthur," said Mother and Father.
"Maybe now we'll get a little peace and quiet," D.W. said. "I'm sick of homework and spelling."

From backstage Arthur could hear the whole
school out in the auditorium.

"Well, today's the big day," said Mr Ratburn.
"How do you feel?"

"I feel fine," the Brain answered.

Arthur gulped. "I wish I were still back in bed!"

The head welcomed everyone and explained
the rules.

The Brain had the first turn. He stepped up to the
microphone.

"The first word is fear," said the head.

"F-E-R-E," said the Brain, a little too quickly.

"I'm sorry," said the head. "That's not correct."

"Are you sure?" asked the Brain.

"What dictionary are you using?"

The Brain wasn't the only one to drop out quickly.
The representatives from Miss Sweetwater's and
Mrs Fink's classes were gone in a flash.
Before long only Arthur and Prunella were left.

It was Prunella's turn.

"The word is preparation," said the head.

Prunella looked down at her feet.

"Could I have the definition, please?" she asked after a moment.

"Preparation," the head repeated, "the process of getting ready."

"Of course," said Prunella. "P-R-E-P," she paused,

"E-R-A-T-I-O-N."

"I'm sorry, that's incorrect," said the head.

"Now Arthur gets a chance to spell it."

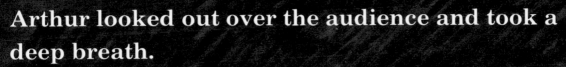

Arthur looked out over the audience and took a
deep breath.
"Preparation," he said. "P-R-E-P-A-R-A-T-I-O-N."
"Correct!" said the head.
Everyone in Mr Ratburn's class cheered.

Then Mr Ratburn went to the microphone. "I'm very proud of Arthur," he said. "In fact I'm proud of my whole class. They worked very hard. This is the last class three I'll have in the spellathon. But next year I look forward to a new challenge . . ."

"Teaching the infants."